MY ROBOT BUDDY
by Alfred Slote

HarperTrophy®
A Division of HarperCollins*Publishers*

My Robot Buddy
Text copyright © 1975 by Alfred Slote
Printed in the U.S.A. All rights reserved.
For information address HarperCollins Children's Books,
a division of HarperCollins Publishers, 10 East 53rd Street,
New York, NY 10022.
Published in hardcover by HarperCollins Publishers.

Library of Congress Cataloging-in-Publication Data
Slote, Alfred.
    My robot buddy.

    "A Harper Trophy book"
    SUMMARY: For his tenth birthday, Danny wants a robot
so he'll have someone to play with.
    [1. Robots—Fiction 2. Friendship—Fiction] I. Title.
PZ7.S635Mz   [Fic]   85-45393
ISBN 0-06-440165-0 (pbk.)

First Harper Trophy edition, 1986.

1

I had no business wanting a robot for my birthday. My folks weren't well off. My father needed a mobile telephone for his solar car. He needed the mobile telephone for business. I needed a robot for pleasure.

My folks and I live out in the country, and after school there was no one my age around. On the Read/Screen I had seen pictures of kids who had robots that acted like brothers and sisters to them. They

1

could talk with them, play ball with them. I wanted to have someone like that, someone I could talk with, throw a ball with, go fishing with, climb trees with.

So I bugged my parents about a robot for a long time. If they talked about the latest line of solar cars, I talked about the latest line of robots. "You know," I'd say, "I saw on the Read/Screen that the newest robots look more like people than people do."

"Is that so, Jack?" Mom would say, and change the subject.

When that didn't work, I'd march around the room pretending I was a robot. Robots have that stiff-in-the-knees walk, and I got so I could robot-walk perfectly.

"Hey, look at me," I'd shout, and march around until Dad would ask me to remember that I wasn't a robot, and couldn't become one no matter how hard I tried, and to please stop shaking the house.

When I wouldn't stop, he would say I looked sleepy.

Which was a cue for bed.

About a week before my tenth birthday, I put on a big "look-at-me-pretend-I'm-a-robot" show, and I got sent up to bed early again. I lay in bed and knew I was being a pest, but I also knew I had to have someone to play with after school, or I'd go nuts.

I guess Mom thought the same thing. I heard her saying downstairs, "Frank, I think we're going to have to get him his robot."

"We can't afford it, Helen," Dad replied. "Nor does he really need one. If *you* wanted a robot to help you with your housework, I could understand that, but just because Jack is bored . . ."

"Couldn't we get one robot that would do both?" Mom was thinking that she could kill two birds with one stone, but I thought that if I ever did get a robot I sure wouldn't share it with anyone else. I got out of bed and tiptoed to my doorway to hear better.

"I don't think so," Dad said. "My guess is that it's fairly simple to program a robot to do jobs, whether they're housework, gardening, or factory work. But to show emotions, hold a conversation, think, be a companion—those are complicated responses, and programming a robot to do things like that must be expensive. I don't think we can afford that kind of robot, Helen."

"All right, Frank, then I think we ought to move back to the city where Jack can have other children to play with."

Now Mom was hitting Dad where it hurt. He hated cities. He hated the feeling of people crowding him. He hated driving in traffic. Dad had grown up in Metropolis III in the northeast, and after college he had worked as an engineer on a space shuttle. When he'd made enough money, he had bought our house in the country, away from modern life and other people. He said people who lived in cities were growing soft. He wanted me to chop wood and dig gardens and climb trees. I didn't mind country life, except that I was lonely. I didn't want a robot to do my chores for me. I just wanted someone to play with.

"Helen," Dad said downstairs, and I could tell from the way he said Mom's name that he was weakening, "buying an expensive robot means no mobile telephone for my car. It means my business won't get bigger. That means constant trips to the home office to report in orders, which means less time that I can spend at home."

"Frank," Mom said, "measure your business against your son's happiness."

Dad was silent a moment. "You're right," he said at last. "We'll buy him his robot."

I clapped my hands and started to shout with happiness, but I had the sense to shut up.

"What was that?" Mom asked.

"Probably a branch falling on the roof," Dad said, as I tiptoed back to bed.

The next day Dad asked me if I wanted to take a tour of a robot factory on Saturday. Saturday was my birthday.

"A tour?" I asked innocently. "What for?"

"Well," Dad said casually, "you're always talking about robots. Perhaps it'll cure you to go through a place that makes them."

"Suppose it doesn't cure me."

"I'll take that chance," Dad said.

On Saturday, Mom, Dad, and I drove in Dad's solar car to Metropolis VII. Metropolis VII is a small satellite city that had been moved down from the northeast after a pollution crisis and rebuilt by the river. Mom liked it. She liked the shops and the parks and the theaters and the art we saw along its moving sidewalks. Even the industrial section was pleasant to drive through. Trees had been planted everywhere.

Dad drove up one ramp and then another, and in a few moments we saw a big sign that said:

ATKINS ROBOTS, INC.
THE VERY BEST IN ROBOTS

Behind the sign was a circular white building.

"Here we are," said Dad.

It didn't look the way I thought it would. I had expected something much larger and straighter, like the factories where solar cars and spaceships are made.

We drove up the ramp right into the building and came to a sign that blinked:

STOP

Dad stopped the car.

The sign then blinked:

LEAVE YOUR MOTOR ON

Blink:

NOW LEAVE THE CAR

"Why, they're treating us as though *we* were the robots," Mom said with a nervous laugh.

"It looks pretty efficient," Dad said.

As we got out of the car, a door to the building opened and a man in a chauffeur's uniform came toward us. He had that stiff-in-the-knees walk. He was a robot.

"You may go inside, if you please," the robot-chauffeur said. "I will park your car."

We watched the robot-chauffeur get in our car and drive it away smoothly.

"I would never have known except for how he walked," Mom said. "Now what do we do?"

"We go inside, just as he told us," Dad said. He looked at me. "Excited, Jack?"

"Yes, aren't you?"

Dad nodded. "I'm curious, I'll confess."

We went through the door the chauffeur had come out from, and we found ourselves inside a green room. There was a desk in the middle of it, and behind the desk was a blond lady in a white uniform. On her uniform was a small red label that said: ATKINS ROBOTS, INC.

She smiled brightly at us. "May I help you?"

"We're the Jameson family," Dad said. "I made an appointment for a tour."

"Of course. Won't you be seated? Dr. Atkins himself will give you the tour."

She checked our name on a list, took a piece of paper out of a drawer, and then left the room, walking stiff in the knees. "Hey," I whispered. . . .

"We know," Mom said.

"There probably isn't a human being in the place," Dad said.

"I wonder if Dr. Atkins will turn out to be a robot," I said.

"It's scary," Mom said.

"I like it," I said.

Dad smiled. "Well, it's a form of living advertising."

"If you can call it living," Mom said.

"I can, and I do," said a voice behind us. We all turned. Standing there was a tall, thin man wearing a green smock and carrying a clipboard with papers on it.

"When robots are well built and well programmed they have lives of their own," the man said in a cold, dry voice. "And who is to say really whether a human being in his humanness is any more alive than a well-programmed Atkins robot in his ro-botness?"

He looked right at me as he asked that, but I wasn't going to answer him. For one thing, I didn't know if he was a robot or a human.

"A human," he answered my unspoken thought, and that gave me goose pimples. "I am Dr. Atkins. And you, I take it, are the Jameson family. If you will please follow me, we will begin our tour of the factory."

We followed Dr. Atkins into a small room in which were three chairs facing a blank white wall.

"Please sit down."

Dr. Atkins stood next to a side wall that had a panel of buttons on it.

The lights in the room grew dim.

"Our factory is made up of five *P* departments: PRODUCTION, PROGRAMMING, PHYSIOGNOMY—"

"What's that mean?" I whispered to Mom.

" 'Physiognomy' means 'face,' " Dr. Atkins said. He had good ears all right. "It is

11

clear that the education of children these days leaves much to be desired. The fourth *P* is PERSONALITY, and finally there is the POWER department. We will now begin the tour."

He pushed a button. It was completely dark in the room now. Suddenly the wall in front of us began to move. What kind of tour was this? I had thought we would go through the factory. But here the factory appeared to be moving while we were sitting still. The wall now seemed to be melting in front of our very eyes. We were looking right through it into a long room. In the middle of the room was a conveyor belt with robots lying down on it. Standing above them, working on them, wiring them, soldering connections, attaching terminals, were other robots. Robots were manufacturing robots!

"In PRODUCTION," Dr. Atkins's voice rang out, "we construct the outer shells and the inner hardware. Atkins Robots,

Inc., produces fifteen robots per day. Not many compared with the output of large factories, but we take pride in the quality of our custom-made, long-lasting, lifelike-appearing robots."

Suddenly PRODUCTION disappeared. The wall was dim again, and the factory once more appeared to move behind the screen.

"We are now coming to our second *P* department—PROGRAMMING."

A scene lighted up in front of us. Seated at a row of machines with keyboards were a dozen older people punching out computer data cards.

"These people are your computer experts, I take it," Mom said.

"You are half-right, Madam," Dr. Atkins said. "They are computer experts, but they are not people. They are robots. Our most expensive robots. We have programmed them to program other robots. These PROGRAMMING robots are *never* allowed to leave the factory. We keep them under

13

lock and key at all times. Robotnapping has become very widespread, and the ransom we would have to pay a robotnapper to get a PROGRAMMING robot back would be exorbitant."

Dr. Atkins paused. "That means 'very expensive,' young man."

"Thanks," I said.

PROGRAMMING disappeared. The factory appeared to glide along behind the wall again.

"Now we are coming to PHYSIOGNOMY—which means, young man?"

"Faces," I said.

"Very good. Suppose you wanted a robot as a companion. What kind of face would you like your robot to have?"

I knew what was going on. I was going to pick out a face for my birthday present.

"Can I see some?" I asked.

I saw more than some. So many faces flashed on the screen, I couldn't keep up with them. There were boy faces and girl faces. Funny-looking faces and good-looking faces. Faces with pug noses, long noses, big ears, little ears, buckteeth, little teeth, no teeth; redheads, blonds, dark-haired kids. Freckles, pimples . . . it was as if every face you ever saw in your life was passing in front of your eyes, and never the same face twice.

"Do you see any face you like, Jack?" Mom asked.

"Lots," I said. "Hey, there's a swell face."

The face I liked held still on the screen. It was a boy who looked about my age. He had red hair and freckles. He was grinning. It was a friendly face.

A light flashed on the screen and then a voice said, "Physiognomy pattern A-1-Y17."

"Is that his name?" I asked.

The screen went black.

"That is his facial pattern," Dr. Atkins

said. "The person who buys him names him."

The factory views began moving across the screen again.

"What kind of name would you give to that face, Jack?" Mom asked.

"I don't know. 'Bob' . . . no, he doesn't look like a Bob. Red-haired, freckles, grinning . . . I've got it—'Danny!' That's a good name for a redhead with freckles. Danny!"

"Danny One," said Dr. Atkins.

"One?"

"In case he gets rebuilt—or, what is more likely, robotnapped. The owner may want a similar model."

"Is there insurance against robotnapping?" Dad asked.

"There is," said Dr. Atkins, "but because there's been so much robotnapping lately, the rates have gone way up. I think that a careful robot owner should have no problem. We are now arriving at our

plained, "a bill is sent to the owner. Naturally, emergency charges are not included in the original price of our robots."

"Naturally," Dad said with a sigh.

"However, if you look after your robot, this should not happen."

"You are receiving now, Vic II," said the POWER department robot in our earphones.

"I am receiving now. Thank you, POWER department," said Vic II.

"Every Atkins robot has a built-in two-way radio so it can communicate with POWER in emergencies. The radio is a simple affair with an on-off button located on the robot's belly."

"A belly button!" I exclaimed.

"Precisely," Dr. Atkins said dryly. "In humans the belly button serves no purpose but to catch lint. For robots, it is a communication source. Our tour is over."

The images behind the walls stopped.

The lights went on. The room was the same as when we had started. Which was no surprise, since we'd never left it.

"Are there any questions about Atkins robots?" Dr. Atkins asked us.

I had a question all right, but it wasn't for Dr. Atkins. It was for Mom and Dad. It was: When do I get my robot? But I was afraid to ask it. These were really expensive robots. Now I understood why. And Dad really needed a mobile telephone for his solar car.

Suddenly there was a knock on the door.

"Come in," Dr. Atkins said.

The door opened. A red-headed kid with freckles was standing there. He had a paper in his hand.

"Happy birthday, Jack," Mom said.

"Happy birthday, Jack," Dad said.

They were both smiling at me. I stared at the red-headed kid.

"Happy birthday, Jack," the kid said, grinning. "I'm Danny One. Here's my printout, Dr. Atkins. I hope he likes me."

"I'm certain he will, Danny One," Dr. Atkins said. "After all, it isn't given to every ten-year-old boy to create a friend. Now, let's check this over . . ." Dr. Atkins examined the paper Danny had given him. "According to the printout, Danny One is programmed to play baseball. He bats right and throws left. In football, he can punt, kick, and throw a pass. He knows how to tackle and block. He is not a fast runner."

"I'm a little stiff in the knees, Jack," Danny said apologetically.

I laughed. "Hey, he's for real."

"He is a real robot," Dr. Atkins corrected me. "Programmed also to play basketball, climb trees, fish, and carry on general conversations. He has been programmed for a fourth-grade education in geography, arithmetic, history, and spelling. He can also do light chores around the house . . ." Dr. Atkins looked at me severely. ". . . Like any well-mannered ten-year-old boy. Ahem.

"Happy birthday, young man. May you enjoy your robot friend Danny One. Take good care of him and, above all, guard him from robotnappers, who are, alas, far too numerous in our world today. Mr. Jameson, may I have your money number, please?"

Dad sighed and took his money number out of his wallet. Danny One and I stood there grinning at each other.

This was both our birthdays.

Down, down the winding ramps we went, driving away from Atkins Robots, Inc. Danny One and I sat in the back seat.

"How does it feel to be just born?" I asked him.

"I don't know, Jack. I don't even know what being born means. I was made."

"Well, I was born, but I can't remember anything until I was about three years old. Then I can remember being on Dad's shoulders and bumping into a door frame. I wonder what your oldest memory will be."

"Everything," Danny said cheerfully. "I've got a memory bank and everything goes into it. I never forget anything."

"You'll be a whiz at school."

"There's not much point in Danny's going to school, Jack," Dad said. "He's been programmed for fourth grade. He knows everything a perfect fourth grader should know at the end of the school year."

"Then I wish you could take tests for me," I said.

Mom laughed. "Danny will do nothing of the sort. Well, you'd better say good-bye to your birthplace, Danny."

We were leaving the last ramp. Danny turned. "Bye, bye, birthplace," he said, smiling.

Mom and I laughed. Dad didn't. He kept looking in the rearview mirror. I guessed he was looking at Danny and thinking about the mobile telephone he couldn't have.

"Jack," Mom said, "why don't you tell Danny about our house and where we live?"

"Oh, I know where you live, Mrs. Jameson," Danny said. "You live on a dirt road, one of the last dirt roads left in Region III. And you live about a mile from Jack's school. You have an old-fashioned white house with a garden outside that you dig yourselves, and there's a pond behind the garden with real fish in it, and there's a big apple tree that Jack loves to climb."

Mom and I just stared at him. "How'd you know all that?" I asked.

Danny grinned. "They programmed your family into me, Jack. They want me to feel right at home."

"Absolutely amazing," Mom said. "But from now on, Danny, you must say 'our' family. Isn't that so, Frank?"

"I don't know, Helen," Dad said, a little absentmindedly. "I'm not sure a robot can really become part of a family. Danny is a machine. A human-appearing machine, but, nevertheless, a machine."

"But, Dad, he's programmed to be my buddy. He's got to be part of the family. He's going to look after me and I'm going to look after him."

Again Dad looked in the rearview mirror. I wished he would quit looking at Danny like that.

"Jack," he said, "I don't expect Danny will be able to look after you any more than this car looks after me. I look after this car. And, in the same way, you'll have to look after Danny. You'll have to make sure his batteries are charged; you'll have to make sure all his parts are in working order. Danny is a machine, Jack. He can't be a member of our family."

"But maybe he'd like to be." I turned to

Danny.

"Jack," Dad said, "he wouldn't like to be what he knows he cannot be. Robots know their limitations. Don't they, Danny?"

"Yes, sir," Danny said.

It made me angry. "Well, if Danny can't be one of us, maybe I'll become like him, I'll become a robot."

Dad thought that was funny. Danny and I weren't laughing.

"Well, Jack, all that proves is that human beings don't know their limitations."

"And a good thing, too," said Mom, "or we'd never have progress. Danny, what else did the computer tell you about our family? I hope it didn't tell you about all our faults."

Danny smiled. "It told me you were a great cook, Mrs. Jameson."

Mom blushed with pleasure. "Well,

you'll be able to decide for yourself as soon as we get home. We're having a little birthday party for both of you, and I've made a big chocolate cake."

"I . . . uh . . . don't eat, Mrs. Jameson," Danny said.

"Oh," Mom said stiffly, "of course."

"Eating's no fun anyway," I said. "I just eat to get energy to play ball and climb trees. You can do that."

"You bet," Danny said cheerfully. "I'm programmed for sports and for climbing trees."

"Then you can climb trees after the party," Mom said. "But we'll have to get you some old clothes, Danny. Dr. Atkins just sent you with the shirt and pants and shoes you're wearing."

"Mom, we can share clothes. We're the same size. We can always share clothes."

"I'm afraid not always," Dad said.

"You're going to grow, Jack. Danny won't."

"Oh." I looked at Danny. "You mean you're always going to be the same size you are now?"

I was wondering how we could be buddies if he stayed small and I got big.

"Well, I could grow, Jack. All my rods have sockets for extender rods, and Dr. Atkins could make me as big as you want each year."

"Hey, you could become a star basketball player. You could be eight feet tall."

Danny laughed. "That's one reason they don't let robots play sports professionally, Jack."

"Gee, if you only could, though. You could be eight feet for games and six feet the rest of the time. Wouldn't that be terrific?"

"The other team would put robots in too

right away," Dad said, glancing in the rearview mirror again, "and then there wouldn't be much sport. It would just be technology competing against technology."

"Dad, can't you stop thinking of Danny as a machine? You keep looking at him in the mirror as though he were just a hunk of nuts and bolts and—"

"I'm not looking at Danny, Jack. There's a car that's been behind us since we left the factory. He's had plenty of time to pass us since we left the ramps, and I wish he would."

I turned. There was a blue solar car behind us with a man at the wheel.

"Some people have no manners," Mom said.

I was relieved that it wasn't Danny Dad had been staring at all this time. "Anyway, we could make Danny grow bigger with me, couldn't we?"

"I'm afraid that's out of the question,"

Dad said. "It's very expensive to keep making a robot bigger. If I had a mobile phone and business impr—"

Whoosh. The blue solar car was alongside us. The driver looked at Danny and at me. There was something about his face that scared me a little. Something hard. Then he speeded up and was gone.

"Wasn't he the curious one?" Mom said.

"I'm glad he's gone," Dad said. "I hate the idea of someone following me. I was beginning to imagine things."

"What things?" Mom asked.

"Oh . . . just things." Dad cleared his throat. "Anyway, Jack, we've spent all the money on your Danny that we can afford. Now we've got to start saving for a mobile phone for this car. I'd like my business to improve. I'd like to be able to spend more time at home with you and Mom."

"And Danny," I said.

"And Danny," Dad agreed, but I knew

he didn't mean it. He would never see Danny as anything more than an expensive toy for me.

And perhaps he was right. Perhaps I'd done the wrong thing, begging so hard for them to buy me a robot. If so, what could I do to make up for it? I couldn't think of a thing.

3

And then we were home.

"Well, Danny," Mom said, "here we are. Is it what you expected?"

"Yes, ma'am," Danny said. "There's the apple tree all right."

"We can climb almost to the top and see for miles around," I said. "C'mon, let's go."

Dad laughed. "There'll be time for climbing *after* the party, Jack."

"Frank," Mom said, "it will take me at

least fifteen minutes to get ready. You boys can climb the tree, but try not to get your pants dirty. Both of you."

As far as Mom was concerned, Danny was part of the family already.

"Let's go," I said. "We've got time to check out the pond. Follow me."

I jumped out of the car and ran down the path to the pond, but Danny couldn't keep up with me. I stopped and waited for him. He was running stiff in the knees, grinning. "I'm coming, Jack," he called.

He really was good-natured. How they had programmed that into him, I didn't know, when they still couldn't make him a fair runner—even for a heap of money.

We walked down the path and I showed him the pond. "There's lots of fish in there, too. Catfish and sunnies and some perch. You're programmed to fish, aren't you?"

"Yes," he said, "worm and fly. I can even go trout fishing."

"Hey, *I've* never done that. Maybe you

can teach me that. Won't that be something? That will make Dad sit up and take notice."

Danny frowned. "I don't know, Jack. Every time your father looks at me he's going to be thinking about that mobile telephone."

"He'll get over it. We'll think of some way to help him get over that. There's the best tree in the world to climb. Let's go."

And once again I started off at a run, and once again I waited for him. But he was really good, going up that tree. Being stiff in the knees even helped him a little. It gave him a tighter grip on the trunk, shinnying up. We passed lots of apples.

"Don't take any of these," I said. "The ones at the top are the best."

We climbed up to the last good-sized branch, and then I went out on it.

"Careful, Jack," Danny said, looking worried.

"Hey, man," I said, "*I*'m supposed to look after *you*. Come on, it's safe."

If there was one thing I knew about, it was this old apple tree. I'd been climbing it as long as I could remember. I moved over and made room for Danny. I wanted him to see the view.

"See the road winding?"

"Yes."

"That's the road we came on. I take it to school every morning. You can see the top of the school from here . . . it's that little bit of white, way down between those trees."

"I see it."

"Over there's the river. It was radioactive till a couple of years ago, but it's clean now. And you can almost see Metropolis VII . . . way, way out there."

"I see it," Danny said.

"And past that—hey, here comes a car."

It wasn't often that cars came down our road. Our house was the only one on it. We heard the solar hum before we saw the car, and then it appeared in front of our house, going slowly, and kept going. It was a big blue car, and it looked just like the one that had passed us on the way home from the factory.

"You don't suppose that's the same blue car," I said.

"It could be. It's the same model."

"There must be lots of those, though we don't see them around here much."

We couldn't see the driver. The car disappeared around the bend in the road.

"Just as well he kept going," I laughed. "Dad would look out the window and start thinking how much he wanted a car with a mobile phone."

"I just wish there was some way he could have a phone," Danny said.

"Well, there isn't, and don't think about it. Dad's bark is worse than his bite. He'll get to like you. I know he will."

"I sure hope so."

"Jack," Mom called out. "Danny. Come on in. Jack and Danny!"

"We're coming," I yelled back. "Let's grab our apples now, Danny."

I slid out a little more on the branch and then, belly down, I reached for two good-sized apples. Then I slithered back.

"We better eat them on the ground. Here's yours."

Danny smiled. "Thanks, Jack, but—"

"That's right! Well, take it anyway. Maybe you can just taste it, even if you can't really eat it."

"I'm not programmed to taste things, Jack. There wouldn't be any point to it."

"Well, take it anyway. We gotta get down."

We climbed down. Danny jumped the last few feet to the ground, and then I did too. I wiped my apple on my pants. Danny watched me.

Then I bit into it.

"Does it taste good?"

"It's great. Bite yours."

"It'd be silly, Jack. I'd just ruin the apple."

"Bite it. You never know. Maybe you've got taste buds."

"I don't, Jack."

"Try. What've you got to lose? First, wipe the apple."

Danny wiped the apple on his pants the way he'd seen me do. Then he hesitated, but I nodded and he took a big bite. He had good white teeth.

"Now chew."

"I'm chewing."

"Well?"

He looked sad.

"Can you swallow?"

He shook his head.

I was sad too. He looked so much like a real person . . . and suddenly he wasn't. He spit out the apple.

"Heck, that's OK. And these aren't such good apples either. They're not half as good as watermelons which—" I stopped. How dumb could I be? If he couldn't taste an apple, he couldn't taste a watermelon. "—aren't any good either. The thing apples are best for is throwing."

I wound up and threw my half-eaten apple as far as I could. It was a good throw. I've got a strong arm.

"Now you," I challenged him.

Danny grinned. He wound up and threw that apple a lot farther than I'd thrown mine.

"Way to go," I said. "If we can form a ball team at school this year, you'll play too. The outfield. Or pitch, even."

Danny laughed. "Robots aren't allowed to play organized sports with humans, Jack."

"Who says?"

"It wouldn't be fair. We never get tired. We're programmed to hit perfectly, to field perfectly, to do everything perfectly except run. But even if I can't play on your team, I can practice with you, and when there are games I can carry the equipment bag and things like that."

"I won't let you do that, Danny. You're my friend, not my servant."

"But I'd like to help."

"Only if I can help you too."

Danny shook his head. "Robots sometimes need repairs, but we never need help, Jack. Unless our batteries run down. Even then we can always call in for a charge. I don't think there's any way you could help me."

"I could protect you from robotnappers. Dr. Atkins said there were lots of them around."

Danny looked around and smiled. "Not around here, I don't think."

"Jack!" Mom called. "Danny!"

"We're coming. We better hurry, Dan."

I took off and ran . . . I kept forgetting Danny couldn't keep up with me. So once again I waited, and when we got back to the house Mom said, "What took you so long? Well, never mind; go and wash up now."

"This way to the bathroom, Danny."

"I've never washed before."

"Let's see your hands."

Danny's hands were as real-looking as mine. They were plastic, of course, but you couldn't tell that from looking or touching. What a great job they'd done when they made him. There was even some dirt from the apple tree bark on his palms.

"A little soap and water," I said. I washed up and Danny watched me. Then he washed up too.

Then we went into the dining room. As we crossed the threshold we were greeted by a song. Mom and Dad sang, "Happy birthdays to you. Happy birthdays to you. Happy birthdays, Jack and Danny, happy birthdays to you." We all laughed. There were four place settings on the table, and a big chocolate cake with ten candles on it.

"What I want to know is, who blows it out?" Dad asked, smiling.

"We both do," I said. I looked at Danny. "You can blow, can't you?"

"You bet I can," Danny said.

"OK, here's what you do. You make a wish and blow."

"What kind of wish?" Danny asked.

"Any kind. You can wish for anything in the world."

Danny nodded seriously.

"Only," Mom added, "you're not supposed to tell your wish."

" 'Cause if you tell it," I said, "it won't happen."

"I got you," Danny said.

"All right," Mom said, "sit down and start blowing."

"First make your wish," I said.

I knew what my wish would be. I wanted Dad not to think of a mobile telephone every time he looked at Danny.

I looked at Danny. He glanced at Dad. *I*

bet he's making the same wish as me, I thought, and winked at him.

He winked back.

"Ready?" I asked.

He nodded.

"One, two, three, blow . . ."

We both blew and the candles all went out.

Mom clapped her hands. "Bravo!"

"Well done," Dad said.

Mom cut the cake and served it. "Tuck your napkin in your shirt, Danny. Like Jack is doing."

"I don't think we have to go that far, Helen," Dad said. "Danny's not going to eat."

Mom blushed. "I forgot. I just got carried away. Danny, you . . . uh . . . won't mind sitting here and watching us?"

"No, ma'am," Danny said politely.

"I bet someday they'll be able to program eating," I said.

"Why would they want to do that?"
Dad asked.

"So Danny could do everything I do."

Dad smiled. "Jack, if Danny did everything you did, he'd be a human and not a robot. As it is, each of you will have experiences the other can't share."

"Like what?"

"Like battery charges, for one."

"Hey, what do they feel like, Danny?"

Danny thought about it a moment. "I don't know, Jack. I've only had one. It didn't feel much like anything. What's the cake taste like?"

"The cake? It tastes like . . . chocolate cake."

"What's chocolate taste like?"

"Why . . . it tastes like . . . you know . . . chocolate. No, I guess you don't know. Anyway, you're not missing that much." I caught myself, embarrassed. "Sorry, Mom, I didn't mean that. Aw, heck, let's go outside and play."

"Finish your cake first," Mom said gently. "Danny's going to be living with us for a long time. And just because *he* doesn't eat food, doesn't mean *you* are not going to. You are, and you're going to enjoy it, too, or I, as the chief cook and baker, will have my feelings hurt. And you don't want that to happen, do you, Jack?"

"No, ma'am," I said, just the way Danny said it. Mom laughed, but Dad frowned. Heck, I thought, if Danny couldn't be like me, I'd keep trying to be like him. Wasn't that part of being buddies?

I gulped down the rest of my cake. "We can go now," I said to Danny. Usually after my birthday cake I opened my presents from Mom and Dad and played with them. Well, Danny was my present, and now I was going to play with him.

As we went out the front door, Dad said, "Danny doesn't know the country, Jack. Look after him, please."

He was still worried about all the money he'd spent.

"OK," I said, "but he'll look after me too. Right, Dan?"

"I'll try," Danny said.

Mom and Dad smiled as though they knew Danny was just being polite.

4

"Sometimes I take a school air-bus, but most of the time I walk," I explained to Danny. "Dad likes me to walk. You'll walk to school with me Monday, won't you?"

"If it's OK with your folks."

"It'll be OK with them. Boy, won't it be fun to fool the kids at school? They'll never believe you're a robot, Dan. You look as real as I do."

Danny smiled. "They'll believe I'm a

robot when they see me walk and run. I'll never walk and run the way you do."

"That doesn't matter, Danny, because I can walk and run just the same as you."

I'd practiced that stiff-in-the-knees walk for months, I'd been so lonely after school. Of course I hadn't thought about it then, but actually I'd been training to be a robot.

"Watch me, Danny," I said, and before he could say a word, I took off down the road, running hard, but still stiff in the knees.

When I stopped and turned, Danny was open-mouthed. Then he said, "Jack, you look just like a robot. Even I couldn't tell the difference. But I can't robot-run that fast."

"You can if you practice. You've got to practice. You've just got to keep running. Like this . . ."

I kept going down the road, running stiff in the knees, hoping he'd follow me. I was teaching a robot to run like a robot! I ran hard, following the curve of the road. In a second my house was out of sight, and so was Danny. I slowed down a little so Danny could catch up with me. It was then that I saw it, parked at the side of the road, almost hidden by some bushes.

The same blue solar car we'd seen from the apple tree.

It was empty. What was it doing here? What had happened to the driver?

I started toward the car to see what I could find out when suddenly, out of nowhere, a pair of arms fastened around me. I was lifted off my feet.

"Hey," I yelled.

"Take it easy," a nasty voice growled in my ear. "You better not struggle or I'll yank out your computer pack."

"Let me go!" I yelled.

A hand was clamped over my mouth, and the next thing I knew I was being carried like a sack of potatoes toward the car.

"I'll let you go, all right, as soon as your owner pays what you're worth," the man growled. "Now quit struggling, robot, or you'll only get yourself broken, and you won't be any good to yourself or me."

It dawned on me then what was happening. I was being robotnapped! I squirmed to get a look at the robotnapper. It was the man who had been driving the blue car that had passed us on the highway. He must have followed us from the factory. And then he had passed us so we wouldn't get suspicious. But then he'd found out where we lived and had waited for a chance at the robot . . . only he had caught *me*.

"Now you're being sensible, robot," he said to me, thinking that because I was quiet I had given up. "Nothing will happen to you if you behave."

He had to take his hand away from my mouth to open the car door. When he did, I said, "Mister, you're making a mistake. I'm not a robot. I'm a human being."

The robotnapper laughed. "Buster, I just watched you run down the road. No human being runs like that. I saw you leave the factory. Now, you just get in here, and all your wires will stay right in place."

"I swear to you I'm not a robot."

"My, oh, my, they're making them smarter and smarter," the robotnapper said admiringly. "Now they're programmed to talk themselves out of trouble. So much the better for your ransom. Now get in there!"

I opened my mouth and yelled as loudly as I could, "Danny! Help! Help! Help!"

"I'm coming, Jack," came Danny's cry from down the road. The robotnapper turned. Around the curve in the road, running as hard as he could, running the only way he knew how, came Danny One.

"Well, I'll be . . ." the robotnapper muttered. "There's another one!"

To my surprise, Danny stopped running. He wasn't coming to help me after all. He stood there, about fifty feet from us, rubbing his hand nervously over his belly.

"Danny," I yelled.

"Let him go," Danny called to the robotnapper. "He's not a robot. He's a human being. I am the one you want. I am the robot. I am one of Dr. Atkins's most expensive robots."

"By gum, you are at that," the robotnapper said. He let go of me and started to go for Danny. Danny began running away, but he ran so slowly that I knew it would be only seconds before the robotnapper caught up with him.

"Hey, mister," I shouted, "he's tricking you. He's just pretending to be the robot. I'm really the robot. Look at me."

The robotnapper turned to look at me. I walked around in a circle, stiff in the knees, more like a robot than any robot ever walked.

The robotnapper scratched his head. He couldn't make up his mind.

"I'm the best robot Dr. Atkins ever made," I said. "I'm programmed to run for hours at a time."

That did it. The robotnapper started back toward me.

"He's not Dr. Atkins's best robot," Danny yelled. "I am. I was programmed to be a friend, to think, and to laugh. I was programmed to be happy!"

The robotnapper hesitated again. He didn't know which of us to grab, and he knew that two at one time would be too much for him to handle. Meanwhile we both went on yelling at him, not giving him time to think. It was a good trick, but how long could it last? Till Dad wondered what had happened to us and came out looking for us? That could be a long while yet. Before that happened, the robotnapper could decide to catch up with one of us and with a knife see which of us had blood, which had wires. Something had to happen.

And something did.

Only it took me a while to catch on.

In fact, the robotnapper realized something was happening before I did. He stopped running back and forth looking at us and instead looked up at the sky.

And it was then that I heard the high-pitched hum of a police air cruiser. We didn't get many police air cruisers in our part of the country, but here was one coming now, flying low, a green and white vehicle. I didn't know what had brought it here, but if only they could see us . . . I began to wave my arms and shout, "Here! Help! Police! Down here!"

I couldn't really believe they'd hear me, but suddenly the air cruiser started its descent onto the road.

That put the robotnapper into action. He ran for his car. Then he took another look at the air cruiser, which, flaps down, was coasting along the dirt road, three feet off the ground, coming at him. He realized his only hope was to get lost among the trees. He jumped into the woods and started running. Danny and I just stood there frozen, watching.

He didn't get very far. Two policemen landed the cruiser, jumped out, and ran into the woods after him. They caught up with him in a few seconds and pulled him back onto the road.

He didn't look half as scary being hand-cuffed by the policemen.

I went over to Danny. "Are you OK?"

"Yes," he said. "Are you?"

"Yeah. But I sure was scared."

"Dr. Atkins warns all his robots about robotnappers. I just never thought I'd meet one so soon."

"Me either. What luck the police were patrolling our dirt road. They never come by here. What incredible luck." We watched the police put the robotnapper into the air cruiser.

One of the policemen walked over to us. He looked at me and then at Danny and then back at me. "Which one of you is the Atkins robot Danny One?"

"He is."

The policeman gave Danny an admiring look. "Good work, Danny One," he said. "If every robot were programmed to think as quickly as you did, we'd be rid of all these robotnappers pretty fast. We've been looking for this guy for a long time. He sometimes makes a practice of following newly purchased robots home from the factory. Well, he won't be following any-one for a long time now . . . thanks to you." The policeman gave Danny a little salute and then went back to the air cruiser.

For the life of me I didn't know why he was congratulating Danny so much. What had Danny done that I hadn't done too? We had worked together to trick the robotnapper. It was just pure luck that the air cruiser was in the neighborhood.

Or was it?

I looked at Danny suspiciously. "What was he congratulating you for?"

Danny grinned. "Well, Jack, I guess . . . this." He pointed to his belly button.

I didn't get it.

"When I saw what was happening," Danny explained, "I knew we couldn't do anything by ourselves and we needed help. So I pushed my radio button and called the factory. I told the Emergency Power Charge robots to call the police and tell them that someone was trying to robotnap me, or you, near your house. That's all I did."

"Well, that was enough. Danny, you are really smart. I never would have thought of it."

Danny laughed. "You just don't have a two-way radio in your belly, Jack, though you do do that robot-run pretty well."

"Too well, I think. Let's go home. Mom and Dad will never believe what happened."

Sure enough, they didn't.

Mom and Dad were sitting in the living room when Danny and I burst in with our tale. They thought we were making the whole thing up: how the guy in the blue car who had passed us on the road had turned out to be a robotnapper and tried to robotnap *me*. And then the idea that Danny had saved me by calling the factory on his two-way radio. . . . Dad had said robots couldn't look after people, and I could tell he thought we were trying to prove him wrong.

"An incredible birthday tale," Dad said, amused.

"Ask Danny if it didn't happen," I said. "Robots always tell the truth."

"All right, Danny. What about it? Is that wild tale true?"

"Yes, sir," Danny said quietly.

Mom turned pale. "You mean, there really was a robotnapper in the neighborhood?"

"Yep, and he almost got *me*. But Danny saved me."

"And Jack saved *me*," Danny said.

"Why, this is the most frightening thing that ever happened to us!" Mom said.

"No, it's not," I said. "It's the best thing. It really proves that Danny and I can look after each other. Doesn't it, Dad?"

"It seems to," Dad said. He looked at us. "Are you both all right now?"

"We're fine, Dad. We really are."

"Good. And now that I know it isn't a wild tale, I want to hear it all over again."

Danny and I laughed. Together we told Mom and Dad the whole thing again: how I ran stiff in the knees down the road, and the robotnapper grabbed me, thinking I was a robot. And how Danny came along and the robotnapper went for him. And how we kept him going back and forth between us until the police air cruiser came. Except that I didn't know it was going to come, only Danny knew because he'd called for help on his two-way radio.

"Well," Mom said, "that was quick thinking."

"Yes, it was," Dad said. "And a darn good thing Danny has a two-way radio built into him." He paused. He cleared his throat. "Tell me, Danny. . . . This radio of yours . . . can you call anyone on it?"

"If I have the right wavelength, Mr. Jameson. At the factory we're only given the wavelength of the POWER department to call in case we need an emergency charge."

"Right. But if I gave you the wavelength of the police, could you call them directly?"

"Yes, sir."

"Frank, you surely don't think this will happen again?"

Dad ignored Mom.

"And if I gave you the wavelength of the fire department, could you call them directly?"

"Yes, sir."

"Dad, you're not counting on us having a fire, are you?"

Dad ignored me.

"And if I gave you the wavelength of my home business office, could you call them directly?"

"Yes," Danny said.

"No!" I yelled, for I finally saw what Dad was getting at. "Danny's not going to be your mobile telephone. He was *my* present, not yours."

Dad laughed. "OK! You're absolutely right, Jack. I was just wondering if I could possibly borrow Danny for five working days. However, if you won't lend him to me . . . that's that."

"Danny would hate being used as a telephone, wouldn't you, Danny?"

Danny shook his head. "No, Jack," he said.

"You mean you want to be used as a mobile telephone?"

"If it would help your dad's business, why not?"

"Well," Mom said, astonished, "not only is Danny looking after Jack, he also wants to look after you, Frank."

"I see that," Dad said. "And I'll admit I wouldn't mind at all being looked after by Danny, but . . . it's up to Jack. Danny was his birthday present and . . ."

Dad didn't have to finish. I knew what he was thinking and so did Mom. I had never shared presents. Being an only child, I never had anyone at home to share presents with. And until now I had never had any presents that my parents would want to borrow.

"All right," I said, "you can borrow Danny, but just for five days."

"Five business days will be all I need, Jack," Dad said happily. "And I'll bring Danny home every afternoon. In fact, we'll both come home every afternoon. I'm betting we'll have more time together: me and you—and Danny."

That settled it. "It's OK with me," I said, "if it's really OK with Danny."

Danny grinned. "It's OK with me, Jack," he said.

Five days turned out to be all the time Dad needed. Every morning that week as I went off to school, Danny drove off with Dad. I learned later that in the car Danny relayed Dad's sales to the home office and received prices and answers on the spot.

When I came home from school every afternoon, there was Danny . . . and Dad. The three of us had fun together. Dad had time now, and he'd get the football out and throw passes to Danny while I tried to intercept. Then he'd throw passes to me while Danny tried to intercept. Mom called the three of us her team.

Friday afternoon though, the last of the five working days, when I got home from school neither Dad nor Danny was there. Mom was out too. I waited outside our house and when Dad finally drove up I sensed something different about the car. It took me a moment to spot the difference—a small antenna on the back.

Grinning, Danny held a mobile telephone out the window.

"Your dad did it, Jack," he said.

"*We* did it," Dad said, getting out. "Jack, if business keeps going well, and I see no reason why it shouldn't, we'll have Danny keep pace with you in growth and education . . . so then you really *will* have a robot buddy."

And that's what happened. Danny went to school with me, and for a while we fooled everyone. When we told them he was a robot, they found it hard to believe.

I sometimes find it hard to believe too. We spend a lot of time together. We do chores around the house, and we play ball and climb trees and fish and hike. At night we talk things over; after I go to sleep Danny gets his batteries recharged.

Sure, there are differences between us: like sleeping and eating and tasting and drinking and feeling . . . but there are lots of similarities too. And we look after each other, the way real friends do. That's the most important thing of all.

Mom and Dad think so too, and so does Danny One Jameson—my robot buddy.